Also by
Marie Winn and John E. Johnson

THE MAN WHO MADE FINE TOPS

A STORY ABOUT WHY PEOPLE
DO DIFFERENT KINDS OF WORK

THE FISHERMAN WHO NEEDED A KNIFE

A STORY ABOUT WHY PEOPLE
USE MONEY

by Marie Winn
pictures by John E. Johnson

SIMON AND SCHUSTER   NEW YORK

First Printing

SBN 671-65101-3   Trade
SBN 671-65099-8   Library
Library of Congress Catalog Card Number: 72-124290
Manufactured in the United States of America

To
Steve and Mike

Long, long ago, people did not use money. Instead, they traded with each other to get the things they needed.

What is trading?

When you say *"I'll* give you my dump truck if *you* give me your kite"—that's trading.

When you say *"I'll* give you my candy if *you* give me your ice cream"—that's trading.

Long, long ago, before people used money, everybody traded different things. A fisherman traded the fish he caught for the other things he needed. A baker traded his bread. A hatmaker traded his hats. A potter traded his pots.

Once upon a time, long, long ago, a fisherman needed a sharp knife. Since there was no
money long ago, he could not go out and buy
one.

So he took one of his fish and wrapped it up to keep it fresh. He took the fish to the knife-maker's house.

"Here is a fresh fish I caught today," he said to the knifemaker. "I will give you the fish if you give me a sharp knife that I need."

"I would be glad to trade with you," said the knifemaker, "but this very morning a man brought me a large fish and traded it for a knife. Now I don't need another fish. What I need is a new hat. My old hat fell into the fire yesterday."

The fisherman took his fish and went to the hatmaker's house.

"Here is a fresh fish," he said to the hatmaker. "I will give you the fish if you give me a hat. Then I can give the hat to the knifemaker and trade it for a sharp knife that I need."

"Sorry," said the hatmaker. "I already have a nice fish for my supper. A boy brought it this morning and traded it for a cap. But I have no more bread in the house. What I need is a crusty loaf of bread."

The fisherman took his fish and went to the baker's house.

"Here is a fresh fish," he said to the baker. "I will give you the fish if you give me a crusty loaf of bread. Then I can give the bread to the hatmaker and trade it for a hat. Then I can take the hat to the knifemaker and trade it for a sharp knife that I need."

"I'm afraid I don't need any fish today," said the baker. "This morning my wife went fishing, just for fun, and she caught an enormous fish. But my best pot has a crack in it. What I need is a new pot."

Once more the fisherman went off with his fish. He went to the potter's house.

"Here is a fresh fish," he said to the potter. "I will give you the fish if you give me a pot. Then I can give the pot to the baker and trade it for a loaf of bread. Then I can take the bread to the hatmaker and trade it for a hat. And then I can give the hat to the knifemaker and trade it for a sharp knife that I need."

The potter looked at the fish. He sniffed it with his nose. He picked it up to feel how heavy it was.

"This is a good fish," he said. "It would make a delicious supper, fried over the fire. I will be happy to trade you a pot for this fine fish."

The fisherman gave the fish to the potter and traded it for a strong, round pot.

The fisherman took the pot to the baker and traded it for a crusty loaf of bread.

Then the fisherman took the bread to the
hatmaker and traded it for a soft leather hat.

At last the fisherman took the hat and went to the knifemaker's house.

He said to the knifemaker, "First I traded my fish for a pot. Then I traded the pot for a loaf of bread. Then I traded the bread for this hat. And now I would like to trade this hat for a sharp knife that I need."

The knifemaker took the hat and tried it on. It fit him very well and kept the sun out of his eyes. He picked out a knife he had made and gave it to the fisherman.

"Here is my best, sharpest knife," said the knifemaker. "But what a lot of trouble you had getting this knife. You had to make so many trades! You had to go to so many people before you found someone who needed your fish!"

"Yes," said the fisherman, "everybody needs *something,* but it's not always a fish that they need."

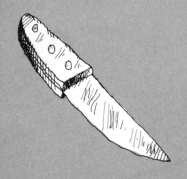

"I have the same trouble," said the knife-maker. "Sometimes I have to make many trades before I get the things I need. Sometimes trading takes so much time that I hardly have time left to make knives."

The fisherman thought very hard and then he had an idea.

"Wouldn't it be good if there were some easier way for us to get the things we need?" the fisherman asked. "Instead of everybody trading different things—fish and pots and bread and knives—wouldn't it be easier if people used one special thing for trading?"

"What kind of special thing could people use?" asked the knifemaker.

"It would have to be something really special, something you couldn't find just anywhere. Otherwise people would not need to work to get it.

"It might be special, colored seashells, or little bits of gold or silver or copper. It might be almost anything, just so long as everyone used the same special thing," said the fisherman.

"That is a fine idea," said the knifemaker to the fisherman. "That is a great idea! We wouldn't have to do all that trading."

"If you gave me some pieces of that special thing, you could get a knife right away. You wouldn't have to make all those trades. I could give some pieces of the special thing to the hatmaker and get a hat right away. I wouldn't have to wait until someone needed a knife to get a hat," said the knifemaker.

"That's it!" said the fisherman. "Everyone would get some pieces of that special thing for the work they do—for the fish they catch or the bread they bake or the pots or knives they make. And then everyone would use those pieces of that special thing to get the things they need—food or clothes or tools."

The fisherman and the knifemaker talked to all the people who lived and worked in their village. They told them their idea.

"A great idea," everybody agreed. "Why didn't we think of it before?"

They picked small pieces of metal to be their special thing for trading. Everybody used the same pieces of metal. And life was much easier and better for everyone.

Today too we use a special thing for getting what we need. Our special thing is also small pieces of metal—pennies, nickels and dimes, quarters and half-dollars. We also use specially decorated pieces of paper called dollars that we can trade anywhere for change—for pennies, nickels, dimes, quarters and half-dollars. We call that special thing *money*.

Money is not good for anything by itself. You can't eat it like bread. You can't wear it like a hat. You can't cook in it like a pot. But it makes it easier for us to get the things we need.

Today a fisherman still catches fish, just as a fisherman did long ago. But a fisherman today sells his fish for money. Then, if he needs a knife, he can use that money to buy a knife.

He doesn't have to trade his fish for a pot, the pot for a loaf of bread, the loaf of bread for a hat, and the hat for a knife, the way a fisherman had to do long, long ago, before people used money.

Suggestions to Parents and Teachers
ACTIVITIES TO REINFORCE THE CONCEPT OF MONEY

1. TRADING GAMES

Distribute pictures of objects of widely varying values (a car, a pencil, a book, a bookcase full of books, an airplane, a marble, etc.). Tell children to pretend that the pictures are real objects; then let them trade with each other. Discuss what is a "fair trade." Why is it not fair to trade an airplane for a pencil? Why are some things more valuable than others?

2. COINS WE USE AND THEIR RELATIVE VALUES

Why do we use a variety of coins instead of one single kind? Show by means of a large container of jelly beans, marbles, etc., priced at a penny a piece, how many pennies are needed to pay for the whole jar. (Do this one by one, letting each child take a jelly bean and put a penny on a pile.) Discuss the

inconvenience of having to carry so many pennies
—leading to the use of nickels, dimes, etc.

Give an idea of the coin equivalents of a dollar
by making piles of coins equal to a dollar—100 pennies, 20 nickels, etc. Why can the large pile of
pennies buy the same amount as the small pile of
quarters?

3. How people get money

Let children act out doing different kinds of work
and use play money to pay them. Discuss why people
get more money for some kinds of work than for
others, due to factors of time, materials and skill.
Then let children use the play money to buy things
at a play store, perhaps using pictures to stand for
real objects.

4. A trip to the bank

Discuss why it is safer to keep money in a bank than
in a jar at home. Discuss paper currency. Why is a
paper bill more valuable than a metal coin, when
metal itself is more valuable than paper? At the

bank, show how you can get change for a paper bill. Discuss other forms of paper currency, such as checks, that still require a backing of money in the bank. What does the bank do with old or damaged paper bills? How does the bank guard against thieves?

5. A TRIP TO A LOCAL MUSEUM OF NATURAL HISTORY

Look at exhibits that show primitive people making clothing, catching fish, curing hides, and bartering. Look at exhibits of different forms of primitive currency—ivory, wampum, shells. Discuss why these were all used as money.

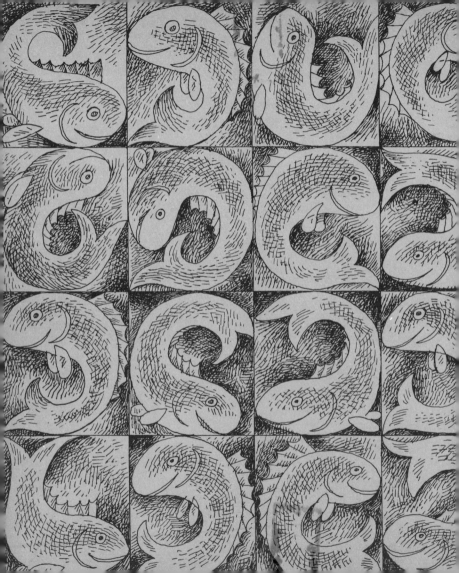